Sindbad's Secret

Sindbad's Secret

Retold and Illustrated by Ludmila Zeman

Tundra Books

First paperback edition published by Tundra Books, 2011

Copyright © 2003 by Ludmila Zeman

Published in Canada by Tundra Books,
75 Sherbourne Street, Toronto, Ontario m5a 2p9
Published in the United States by Tundra Books of Northern New York,
P.O. Box 1030, Plattsburgh, New York 12901

Library of Congress Control Number: 2002110526

Library and Archives Canada Cataloguing in Publication

Zeman, Ludmila
     Sindbad's secret : from the tales of The thousand and
one nights / Ludmila Zeman.
6 and up.

isbn 978-1-77049-265-3

I. Title.

ps8599.e492s565 2011   jc813'.54   c2010-903190-3

We acknowledge the financial support of the Government of Canada through the Book Publishing Industry Development Program (BPIDP) and that of the Government of Ontario through the Ontario Media Development Corporation's Ontario Book Initiative.

We further acknowledge the support of the Canada Council for the Arts and the Ontario Arts Council for our publishing program.

ONTARIO ARTS COUNCIL
CONSEIL DES ARTS DE L'ONTARIO

Medium: pencil, colored pencil, and watercolor on paper

Printed and bound in China

1 2 3 4 5 6   16 15 14 13 12 11

I dedicate this book to Shahrazad — most beautiful teller of fabulous tales.

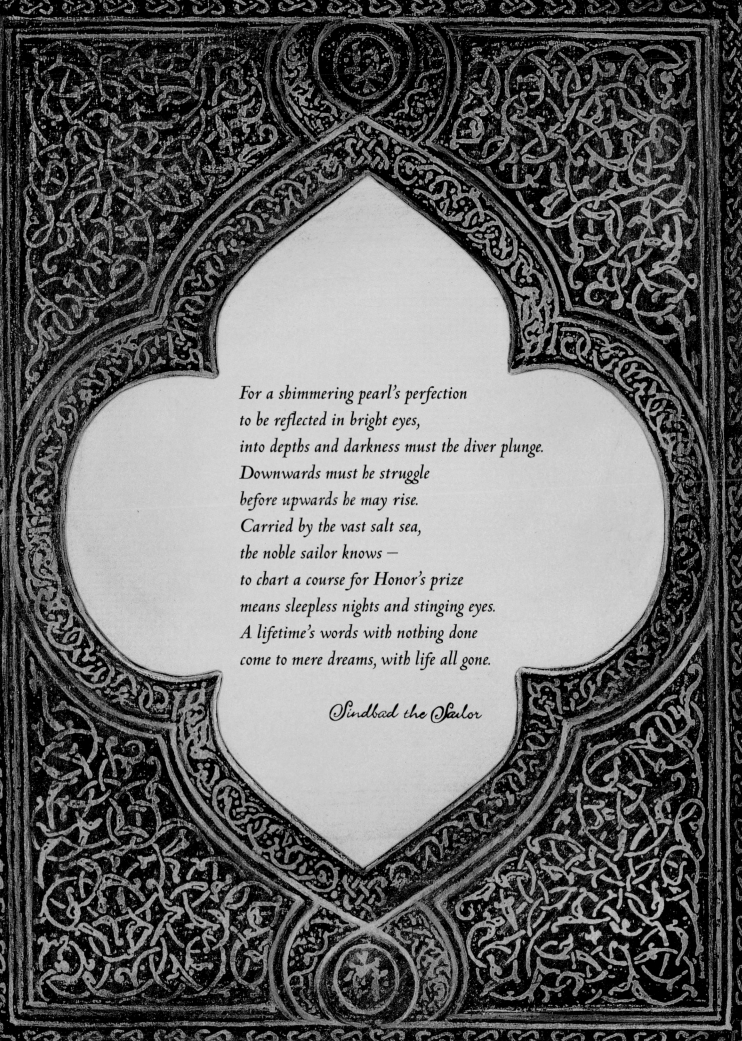

For a shimmering pearl's perfection
to be reflected in bright eyes,
into depths and darkness must the diver plunge.
Downwards must he struggle
before upwards he may rise.
Carried by the vast salt sea,
the noble sailor knows —
to chart a course for Honor's prize
means sleepless nights and stinging eyes.
A lifetime's words with nothing done
come to mere dreams, with life all gone.

Sindbad the Sailor

In the city of Baghdad, during the reign of the great caliph Harun al-Rashid, lived two men identical in name but different in fortune. Sindbad the Sailor was a wealthy merchant who lived in a palace. Sindbad the Porter was but a poor servant. Fate brought them together, and for many days and many nights, Sindbad the Porter listened as Sindbad the Sailor told tales of adventure.

One morning, Sindbad the Sailor ordered a scented bath filled with rose petals and aloe to be prepared for the porter. "You have seen and sampled the comforts of my wealth, including this luxurious bath," he said, "but today I will reveal my greatest secret and show you my finest treasure – the jewel of my last voyage.

After I escaped from the land of giants, I swore never to be sea-bound again. But on the journey home, merry times on the merchant ship made me forget the horrors of past voyages. When we reached Basrah, where I was to leave the merchants and continue home to Baghdad, I convinced them to take me along on their next voyage.

aves and wind propelled us to lands we had never seen before, with beautiful cities filled with wondrous houses and people who spoke in strange languages. They drank scented tea from thin white cups of a fragile matter so exquisite that we exchanged all our goods for their dishes.

We filled the ship beyond its capacity. No one noticed how it creaked and swayed when we left the mysterious land. Even as we sailed the Yellow Sea's treacherous waters, where many ships had disappeared, we rejoiced, blinded by the wealth we had stowed below deck.

Suddenly the sky darkened and violent rain fell. Our ship danced on the sea like a feather in the air. Monster fish and enormous serpents encircled us. A serpent as high as a mountain opened her giant muzzle and slithered towards the ship. Fear so great possessed me that I jumped straight into the roaring waves. I slid underneath the serpent and felt her rubbery skin extending and constricting as she devoured the ship.

1 found myself at the bottom of the ocean, surrounded by fish of splendid colors. They did not appear friendly, eyeing me like a tasty meal! I pushed myself up from the seabed toward air and escape. Just in time, I reached a loose plank from the ship and held on to it for dear life.

Days passed as I floated, the unforgiving sun burning my lips and the salt water eating away at my skin. Finally the waves washed me up on an island.

I slept until the next day, and when I awoke, I was in paradise. Around me plump purple grapes bursting with ripeness glistened in the sun. I collected their sweet juice in the dried-up gourds that lay beneath the trees.

A manlike creature startled me. He waved his hairy arm towards the grapes high up on the vine. I wished to show him kindness, for he seemed quite helpless. But when I hoisted him up to reach the grapes, he tightened his legs around my waist and his arms around my neck, and started beating me with his cane!

leaped from side to side and jumped up and down, but I could not shake him off. For days and nights I carried him like a horse carries his master, obeying every command lest he beat me.

One hot day he ordered me to carry him into the shade of the trees along the shore. There were the gourds of grape juice lying in the sun. I stole a drink. Oh, how refreshing it was! I skipped joyfully with the beast on my back. The creature immediately snatched the gourd from my hands, emptied it in one giant gulp, and, screaming, dug his heels into my sides.

Suddenly I felt his grip loosen and his cries became moans. Hands clutching his head, he fell to the ground like a sack of flour. He was drunk from the juice that had fermented under the sun, and turned into wine. Finally I was freed from this monster!

As luck would have it, a ship was approaching the island. But this was no ordinary ship. It belonged to notorious hunters that mercilessly killed elephants for their ivory tusks.

When the ship landed, the captain summoned me to kneel at his feet and said: 'Men greater than you have perished under the unforgiving cane of the Old Man of the Sea. You are brave, and for that I will rescue you.'

I boarded the ship gratefully, but soon realized that I was taken on the vessel as a slave. I was granted a small carpet on which I was allowed to rest. I accepted my fate and spread the carpet on the wooden deck. I fell into a deep sleep and, when I awoke, I was in the port of a new land. The bright moon lit the lovely city, but the people were mourning, for their beloved Maharajah had died the night before.

The next day I was given a horse and bow and arrow, and I was ordered to follow the hunters into the jungle. As we crossed the city, we passed the Maharajah's magnificent funeral procession. Suddenly, my heart stopped.

hy was the most beautiful girl that I had ever seen bound on top of an elephant? I learned that her name was Fatima and that she was the Maharajah's most beloved dancer. She would die with her master, according to the land's custom. I thought of nothing but how to save her.

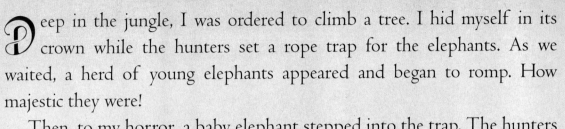

Deep in the jungle, I was ordered to climb a tree. I hid myself in its crown while the hunters set a rope trap for the elephants. As we waited, a herd of young elephants appeared and began to romp. How majestic they were!

Then, to my horror, a baby elephant stepped into the trap. The hunters pulled on the rope with all their might. One of them shouted at me: 'Shoot! Shoot the elephant!'

The poor elephant tugged at the rope, crying helplessly. I could not bear his suffering, and drawing my bow, I pointed an arrow at him.

As I intended, my arrows sliced the ropes and set the elephant free. How foolish was I to have doubted my father, who went to great pains to teach me the noble sport of archery!

Before the hunters realized what had happened, the elephant disappeared into the jungle. They set off after him, cursing and threatening to deal with me later. As I contemplated my fate, I felt the tree shaking. A giant elephant was pulling it up by the roots! Suddenly, contemplating my destiny seemed futile, for now my fate was surely sealed.

I was so frightened that I fell from the tree, unable to run. I expected the elephant's massive trunk, wrapped around my waist, to squeeze the last breath from my body. Instead, she whisked me gently onto her back. When I opened my eyes, thinking that perhaps death was not so painful after all, I noticed the baby elephant skipping next to his mother. I realized that the animal meant me no harm.

We made our way through the jungle towards a distant light. My heart sank when I saw the beautiful Fatima atop the Maharajah's funeral pyre.

I slid down from the elephant's back and ran towards Fatima. The elephant must have understood my intention, for she charged towards the burning pyre. Screams of terror echoed through the jungle when the mourners saw the giant elephant emerge from the dark. They had never seen such an enormous and powerful elephant. Surely this must be an angered god! The elephant scooped up the unconscious Fatima, and placed her gently on top of her back. Then she lifted me up, so I could hold Fatima while we were carried to safety.

How long the elephant ran, or where she was taking us, was of no matter to me, for I held the most precious jewel in my arms.

The noble animal carried us far, far into the depths of the jungle, until the sun was chased away by the silver moon.

I was lost in Fatima's eyes, so smitten by her beauty that I did not notice that we were surrounded by hundreds of ivory tusks. The elephant had brought us to the graveyard, where the stately giants left behind their tusks before entering the elephant afterworld. I looked up at the elephant who brought us here with gratitude for revealing the elephants' ancient secret.

I hid Fatima in the jungle, protected by the elephants, and I returned to the village in disguise. When the master hunter realized who I was, he ordered my head cut off. But I insisted on telling him my story, and he agreed to let me live if this place of tusks existed. I led him to the graveyard and showed him the ivory tusks. He realized that he would become the richest man without ever having to kill another elephant. He promised to grant me any wish.

I requested a ship ready to sail for Basrah by nightfall. He gave me the finest ship I had ever seen and bags of gold to take back to Baghdad.

That night I returned to the jungle, where Fatima was hidden, and brought her to the ship. I immediately ordered the crew to sail to Basrah, and then on to Baghdad.

indbad the Sailor looked at the astonished Sindbad the Porter and said: 'You see, dear Porter, not all is as it seems. You think I have a life of ease, but I have suffered and I have cried to gain the wealth that you see now. And, above all, I have learned that there is no greater wealth and no greater reward than love.'"

Sindbad the Sailor put his arm around his beautiful wife, Fatima, and gazed fondly at the little children at his feet.